—Sgàthach
the WARRIOR QUEEN

Sgàthach the Warrior Queen

Aonghas MacNeacail

illustrated by Simon Fraser

BALNAIN

Published in 1993 by
Balnain Books
Druim House
Lochloy Road
Nairn IV12 5LF

Printed and bound by Posthouse Printing, Findhorn, Scotland

Cataloguing in Publication: A catalogue record for this book is available from the
British Library

ISBN 1 82557 29 5

What a smart young man I was — or so I thought. *I'm a warrior now, I thought, I've been through all the training. I've been through all the tests. There's nothing anyone can teach me now.* And then my father said, *You have so much to learn. Prepare yourself to sail across the sea, until you reach the Isle of Shadows. Sgàthach will teach you everything you need to know. She is more clever than you could ever imagine. Her name means 'Like Shadows'. Remember that, and watch her every move, and you'll become the greatest warrior who ever lived.*

So there I was sailing my curragh up the coast of Skye, dancing my eyes across the land, to see if I could spot the castle where she stayed, this Sgàthach, the "Warrior Queen". **Look out**! the ship nearly tore my boat in two. It had a great sail and oars, but the person rowing it hadn't seen me. I'd never seen its like — long and sleek, made out of shiny wood, as bright as gold, not like my curragh, which was made of deerskins stretched across a frame of hazel branches.

O, it was quite a beast, that boat of polished yellow wood, which slipped across the water like the wind, and — what was that I saw? — It was a *woman* at the oars! I'd heard that such things happened, long ago. It means bad luck, though. I watched her fold the sail away, and cast a net. And as she floated in the shadow of a wall of mountains greater than I had ever seen, I heard the woman *whistle*. That's *never* done at sea. It'll bring the most *terrible* luck to the sailor. Although I was a warrior, fear slithered through me like a sea of snakes.

But as I turned my boat to find a breeze that would take me well away from there before she noticed me — she noticed me. And shouted, loudly, *Hey, my lad, I haven't seen your likeness round these parts before. Who are you, and where in Ireland have you sailed from?* She spoke the way my people did. I turned my boat again, to face her and said *They call me Cù Chulainn — Culann's Hound. I'm here to learn the skills of war from Sgàthach.*

Then search no further, young Cù Chulainn, said the woman, who was tall and handsome, and dressed only in a short brown shift, which left her shoulders bare. *You are Sgàthach?* I couldn't keep a catch of excitement out of my voice. And then I thought of what she had said about my family. *How did you know I came from Ireland?*

By that boat of skins you call a curragh, which looks so frail, yet rides the waves like a bird. Then she pointed to her castle, not far up the coast. *Get yourself some food and rest in the warrior's lodge,* she said, *I'll have to tend to my nets for now, but I'll see you in the morning.*

I'd thought I was the big bold warrior, and I was exhausted after my long voyage, but that night, I could hardly sleep a single wink with excitement. What could Sgàthach be showing me of the arts of war, that I hadn't learned already? Because I wanted to be the very best, she would have to show me something really special.

Next morning, there was a dance in my feet as I strode towards Sgàthach's castle. *I'm going to learn,* I thought, *to be the*

greatest warrior of all! When I came towards the castle entrance, I saw there was a bridge of stone between me and the great oak door, which was open. Sgàthach came out with a smile upon her face, warm and friendly. Eagerly she crossed the arched bridge. *Welcome to Sgàthach's castle* she said, extending her hand to take mine. I did the same. And I heard her say Look into my eyes, although I'm absolutely certain her lips never moved. Next thing I knew was an explosion in my head. I fell, head spinning, no idea what had hit me.

Then I heard her laugh. She was a big woman, but she laughed like a young girl. *You've much to learn about the art of war, my friend,* she said. *You must be a witch!* I said. *No human being struck that blow. There's no-one here but you and me, and you were there in front of me.* She laughed again in such a way I knew it must have been her who struck

my head, but how was she so fast? That
was what I couldn't understand: and that
was what I'd have to find out for myself,
if I was going to be the greatest warrior
of all.

But suddenly she was gone again, and I
was still outside her castle. *I'd better find
her* I thought. Between me and the castle
was a deep ditch, which was crossed by a
bridge that was low at each end and high
in the middle, and the only way in to the
castle. So up to the bridge I stepped.

No sooner did I set foot on the near
end but the other end flew up at me, and
threw me onto my back. I had another
go. It threw me flat again. The third time,
I stepped on the near end, made my special salmon-leap onto the middle and
before the bridge could move, I was right
across.

By now I was quite fed up with this
woman's trickery. So when I found the
gates of the castle were locked, I threw

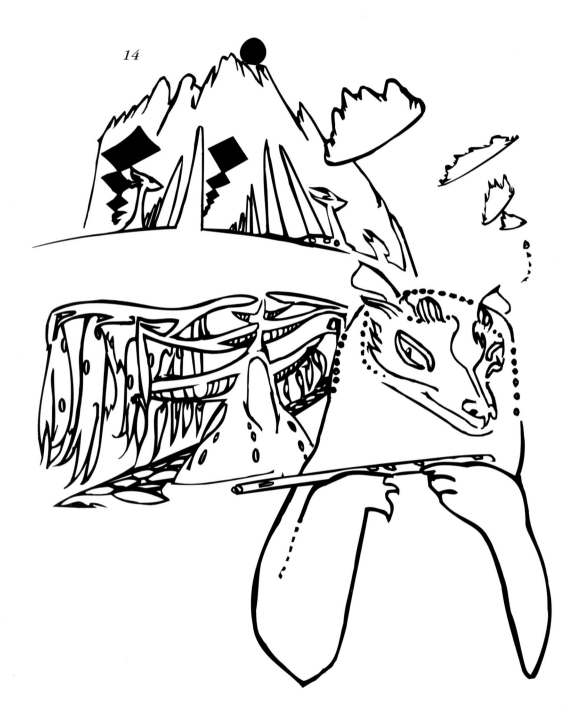

my spear at it, and smashed it through.
Inside, I met a servant girl, but she
wouldn't tell me where I could find
Sgàthach. I took her by the hand, but
then she screamed *You hurt my finger!*
Immediately, the hardest warrior I'd ever
met came leaping at me from a door. We
fought. I killed him. Then I saw Sgàthach
standing by the body, weeping. *He was
the best*, she said. *He was the man who
led my armies into battle. Now he's
dead.* I was sorry for her and for what I
had done. *I'll take his place*, I said. *I'll be
your champion.* She smiled between her
tears, and went back into her own part of
the castle.

We'll have a game of shinty, was the first
thing she said, next time I saw her. Then
she picked up a caman, with its bent end
of hard flat edges, that she had hooked
into her belt, and a hard wooden ball
from a pocket in the front of her dress. I
thought, *This is a waste of time. I'm sup-*

posed to be here to learn the arts of war, and she's asking me to play a game. But I didn't say anything to her — after all we didn't have teams, so how could we play a game like shinty? Then she gave a shriek of a whistle that nearly tore the inside of my ear out! And suddenly we were surrounded by sturdy men with camans in their hands. *Choose your team,* she said. *I'll be watching how you play. A good player will make a good warrior.*

Sgàthach threw her caman to me, then before I had hardly caught it, she threw the wooden ball, as hard as she could, *at* me. I was so angry with her for wasting my time with this silly game, that I swung my caman at the ball with all my might, striking it so hard that it hit the hillside behind her castle like a bullet and churned its way through the belly of the rock, leaving a tail of flaming hot dust behind it. Later, I heard it came out the other side of the hill with such force that

it killed three shepherds and a miller grinding his corn before curving into the sea in a great cloud of steam. Later, I heard that was what made Aoife, the queen of the other side so angry she declared war on Sgàthach. I don't know though. Aoife liked to fight. Sgàthach was brave, but she thought fighting was silly, unless you had a really good reason to fight.

I *do* know that I was nearly in a fight — a really *big* fight, with all the other warriors. They were *furious.* They surrounded me with their camans like raised swords — and suddenly they *became* swords. Just as that circle of steel was about to slice down out of the sky and cut me to pieces, Sgàthach shouted *Stop!* Then she turned to me and said *You! Unless you are prepared to control your temper, and act as if you are part of the team, then there is nothing I can teach you.*

That was all she said. Then she turned to all the warriors and said, *Now let us try you with the apple game,* and from the same pocket that had contained the shinty ball, she took apples, nine for each warrior. And there were *thirty* warriors! That was an awful lot of apples from one small pocket.

What we had to do was juggle our nine apples and never allow more than one to rest in our hand at any one time. First, she showed us how to do it, then she said, *Now let me see you do it.* Of course there were apples falling and rolling all over the place. Soon I was the best juggler there, but even I could only keep four apples in the air at one time. *Sgàthach,* I said, *this is impossible!* But all she said was *Try again.* And we had to keep going while she stood and watched us. Eventually the others got to being able to keep six in the air, and I could manage seven, if I concentrated really hard. At last she said, *You can rest now.*

There were many other games to test us, but every time we learned a new one, we worked even harder at practicing the ones we knew already. My favourites were games like the one where we learned how to balance yourself in the war-chariot when the speed of it bumping across rocky gound was likely to throw you out. Then there was the *breath game*, where you had to blow golden apples up in the air — and keep them there as long as possible, just by balancing them on the jet of your breath.

I learned to do them all. So did most of the other warriors, but Sgàthach never let any one of us feel we were better — or less good — than the others. I was faster at most things than anyone else, but I always had to remember that without the others I might not be much good at all — against an army, say. *Always work*

together, she'd say. Then one day, she announced that she was going to teach all she knew about weapons.

We'll begin with Archery, she said. At the far end of the training field a row of targets had been set up. Each warrior fetched his own favourite bow, and a quiver of arrows. Each warrior drew an arrow from his quiver, and aimed at the target. *No!* cried Sgàthach, *You must pre-pare yourselves.* She took a bow herself, then balancing her feet delicately, raised the bow and drew the bowstring, letting it go without using any arrows at all. The snap and hum it made was like a strange musical instrument. *That will banish evil spirits before we begin our lessons,* she said. Then she notched an arrow on the bowstring, drew the bow, took aim and fired. It looked so easy! I've never seen it look so easy! It was just as if she were stretching her arms after waking up in the morning. And the arrow sped straight

towards the centre of the bull's eye!

Now you try, she said to all the warriors, and we did try, but not one of us was able to hit the bull's eye. *You've got to breath properly*, she said. *Oh*, I said, but it was better, right enough.

Then one day, as we practiced new skill, we were so busy thinking about what we had learned that we didn't pay much attention to a strange noise that crept up on us every now and again. At first it came in short scratches, like sounds carried on a hollow wind. Voices, far away, and metal being beaten. Even Sgàthach was so busy teaching us she didn't seem to notice it. Then one day it got so loud she stopped us — *SSSSHH*! she whispered. *Listen!* We could hear it clear as anything: a woman's voice, and a babble of men's voices —and the sound of metal on metal. We looked all around us but we couldn't see anything. The

noises didn't come from the castle, nor from the seas beyond it, nor from the birchwood behind it. Listen, said Sgàthach again. Then she stretched out her arm and pointed towards the hole in the hillside that had been left by the shinty ball I had hit in my anger many months before. That was where the noises came from.

It's Aoife, said Sgàthach. *She's preparing for war. Against us. Her warriors are sharpening their swords and axes. She blames me for the death of her shepherds and the miller.* Sgàthach looked at me, and there was a terrible sad anger in her eyes. *Now you see the price of your foolish rage*, she said. *Much blood will be shed before this matter can be settled, and many mothers will be weeping for their dead sons and daughters.*

We have little time, before Aoife's armies will come marching on us. Then she gathered us around her, and began to teach us everything she still had to teach us about the art of warfare, so that we might be ready for Aoife's armies. *Prepare to fight before the day is out,* she said, *Aoife's warriors are marching down the strath towards us. We must be up in those hills before noon, if we are to stop her.*

Just before we set off to fight the enemy, Sgàthach called us to a great brass tub brim-full of a golden liquid. Was this magic too? But, *No,* she said, *It's only ale, there'll be no time for any one of you to quench your thirst while the battle rages.* And then she handed each of us a silver cup, into which she poured a ladle-full of the ale. As soon as I supped mine a swirling fog of dizzines rolled around my head, and I slid down into a darkening well of sleep. Then I awoke

and it seemed a moment, just, had
passed. Sgàthach was there watching me. *You've only slept an hour,* she said, *The drug I mixed into your cup would have kept the strongest warriors asleep for a whole day and a night.*

And then I saw that tears were in her eyes. *I drugged you so that you would miss the fight,* she said. *You are too brave for your own good. I did not want to see you killed. But now you are awake, I cannot beg you not to go.* And she was right. For I would go, whatever she had said. Old though she was, with the wounds of many battles in her bones, Sgàthach was off away ahead of me, towards the howl and roar and clatter of battle.

When we got to the battlefield, it was already red and glistening with the blood of warriors. Aoife, the young and beautiful queen of the other side, was as great a warrior as Sgàthach, some said. But young men did not come to her to learn the arts of war, so she was jealous of Sgàthach.

This bloody day she perched upon a rock above the clash and slash of swords, and called on Sgàthach, *Fight me Sgàthach — you and me alone. I've waited long for this — my chance to prove that I am best!*

Oh, I could see that this made Sgàthach furious — an anger so great it would have made her careless in the fight. So I asked her *What does Aoife hold most dear above all else?* And Sgàthach said, *Her two black horses, her golden chariot, and her charioteer.* So then I said *You wait here. I promised I would be your champion. I'll fight her.*

It surely was a fight. I threw a spear at Aoife. She stepped aside and as it passed her, she sliced my spear in two with the

edge of her open hand. I'd never seen the like! I lunged at her with my sword. She smashed it. All I had left was a piece of sword no bigger than my fist. *Look! Look!* I called to her, *your golden chariot and horses and your charioteer have fallen over the cliff! They're all dead!*

Aoife looked around, and straightaway I grabbed her, threw her on my back as if she were a sack and carried her to where our army was. I threw her to the ground, and held my sword against her throat. *Now that I have captured you, you must grant me three wishes, Aoife.* I said. *You must leave some of your warriors as hostage for Sgàthach; secondly, you must promise never to attack her again, and lastly, I want you to give me a son.*

I grant all you ask, said Aoife. That night I went with her. In the morning, she told me we would have a son. I gave her a gold ring for the boy to wear when

his finger was big enough. And then he had to come to Ireland to find me. I told her the name to give him, and she said he was not to tell it to any man. *Nor,* I said, *should he refuse any challenge to fight.*

When I returned to the castle, Sgàthach tended my wounds. When I was better, she said, *I've taught you all I know. It is time for you to return to Ireland.* And she walked with me down to the little sheltered harbour among the rocks where my boat awaited me. She helped m float the boat, and watched as I climbed aboard, and then she called, *Farewell, Cù-Chulainn. You are the greatest warrior I have ever known. Many victorious battles lie ahead of you. But beware of your terrible temper. It will bring you sorrow — one day you will kill your own son.*

As I sailed away, Sgàthach stood on the

rocks, waving to me. Her long hair streamed out behind her, like silver banners. Her deep dark eyes scanned the horizon. She could see things long before they happpened. She was a wise woman — the greatest teacher I have ever known.